## DEDICATION

I've always had a great love for children, and it's been a joy
to have so many of them as fans of our television
show. It is my hope that this story, which
was always a favorite of my own
children, will become a
favorite of theirs.

First printing ----- October, 1977
Second printing -- January, 1978

# LAWRENCE WELK'S
# Bunny
# Rabbit Concert

By Lawrence Welk with Bernice McGeehan

*Illustrated by Carol Bryan*

**YOUTH PUBLICATIONS / THE SATURDAY EVENING POST COMPANY**
Indianapolis, Indiana

*When my children were still very small, I had to be away from them for days and weeks at a time, traveling with my little orchestra. It was so very hard for us to be away from each other in those years! And yet, it just made our time together that much more precious. The moment I came home and opened the front door, my children would come running from all parts of the house, hurling themselves into my arms or clutching me around the knees, as we hugged each other in welcome. And then they'd say—jumping up and down with excitement. . ."Daddy, do you have a new story to tell us, do you Daddy, do you have one?"*

*So always, I tried to have a new story for them. But the odd thing is, that of all the stories I told, the ones they liked best were those about my own boyhood days on the farm, when I was a small child myself. And the one they liked best of all, is the one I'm going to tell you now. . . .*

When I was a small boy, just about your age, I lived on a farm in North Dakota. It was very, very hot in the summer, and very, very cold in the winter, with huge icicles hanging from the window-sills, and great drifts of snow piled up against the sides of the house. Sometimes the snow was so high we could barely tunnel our way out to the barn to feed the animals, and it was so cold we had to stay inside for days at a time.

But in a way, those were the happiest times of all! My mother would keep the kitchen warm and fragrant with good things to eat as she cooked on the wood-burning stove. After dinner we children would sit around the table and play, or gather 'round the pump organ and sing. My brother John accompanied us on the violin or clarinet, while my mother led us in song. She had a lovely voice, and was an exceptionally fine dancer, too, and taught all of us children how to do waltzes and polkas. And on many a long, dark, winter's afternoon, as the horses and cows and sheep dozed in the barn . . .and the fields outside our house lay quiet under the winter snows. . .we children sang and danced together. The house was filled with laughter as my father played the accordion, stamping his foot upon the floor, and whistling the tune at the same time.

But all of that changed in the spring! Then the days were never long enough to do all the work that has to be done on a farm. As the weather grew warm and the snow began to melt, we boys helped father plow the ground which had frozen under the ice and snow. Then we planted the tiny seeds of wheat, and corn and barley. Meanwhile, our sisters helped mother plant a vegetable garden of watermelon, and rhubarb, and squash and onions, and radishes and cucumbers, so we would have food to

store for the long winter months ahead.

Some days, if there was enough time, my brothers and I would go to the nearby lake and trap muskrats. (We could earn a little extra spending money that way.) My dog Rex always went with me. He was a special pal to me, and helped me by rounding up the cattle in the fields and bringing them back to the barn. Rex trotted alongside me wherever I went during the day, and slept on the floor beside my bed at night.

The days were long, and very hard, I suppose. But in a family as large and loving as ours. . .(there were eight of us brothers and sisters). . .you learn very early in life how to share with one another. And even though I was a rather frail and sickly little boy, I was always very anxious to do my full share to help our family.

But one day I became very, very sick, and had to go to the hospital for an operation. For weeks after that, I had to stay in bed at home. I think I felt worse about not being able to do my share of work than I did about being kept in bed! But it did no good to fret, so to pass the time, I practiced "playing" the pump organ, by pretending there was an imaginary keyboard spread out on top of my bedspread. Later, as my strength returned, I practiced on the real pump organ. And still later, I began to play the accordion. And, oh!. . .how I loved its bright and brilliant sounds! I loved it so much I made up my mind I must have one of my own. After that, I spent every spare moment trapping animals so I could earn enough money to buy my own small accordion.

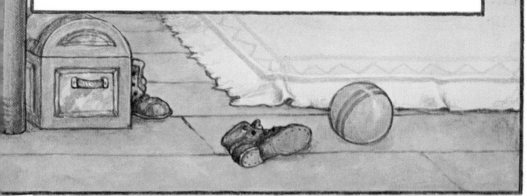

When it arrived, it was the happiest moment of my life! I practiced it by the hour! The moment my chores for the day were finished—I'd start playing. After dinner, I'd play some more. When I went to bed at night, I'd put the accordion on the floor beside me, so I could start practicing early in the morning. As I improved, I began playing for birthday parties in our neighborhood, too. One of my brothers would come along and pass the plate, and people would drop in a penny, or a nickel, or

sometimes even a dime! Then, after the party, I'd go home and play more, more, and more, far into the night. Finally, my family had had enough! "Lawrence," they said, "please! Stop playing! We just can't *stand* any more!"

Oh, my. What to do? I didn't want to bother anyone in my family, of course, so finally I decided to go to the far side of the barn, and play there. No one could hear me, and I could play to my heart's content.

So one fine spring afternoon, just as the sun was beginning to lower and the day's work was done, I took my accordion and a little milking stool, and, with Rex beside me, went out beyond the barn. No one was there—not a soul. I picked up my accordion, slipped on the straps, made a deep bow to my imaginary audience, and then sat down on my little milking stool and began to play some old-fashioned waltzes my dad had played for years.

Suddenly. . .to my surprise. . .I saw I had a visitor! There on the ground in front of me. . . looking up with his bright, inquisitive little eyes, was a bunny rabbit, ears standing straight up, little pink nose twitching. Charmed. . .I watched him as I continued to play, and then, to my astonishment, I saw another little pink nose peeking out from underneath the barn, wiggling and twitching. Then another. . .and another. . .until finally six little bunnies had popped out from beneath the barn and sat with their paws up, listening to me play!

I beamed at my cute little audience, and when I finished I bowed low. "What would you bunny rabbits like to hear now, if you please?" I asked, entranced by their rapt attention.

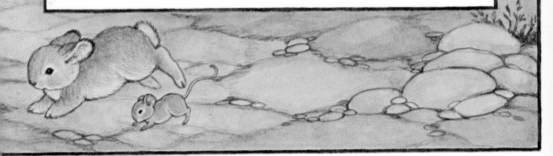

Before they could answer, I swung into a bright and lively polka, and as I played, the birds, swooping lazily about in the soft spring air, began flying over and perching on the roof of the barn so they could hear me better. One of them even came over and lighted on a nearby tree stump, and began to trill and sing right along with me.

Next day, as soon as my chores were finished, I rushed out to play again, wondering if my friends would show up. And sure enough, almost before I got the first notes out, the little pink noses began peeking out from under the barn, sniffing and

twitching, and then the bunnies hopped over to their front-row seats. The birds came flying back to listen again and, to my delight, a whole flock of yellow baby chicks came "cheeping" around the corner of the barn with their mama-hens right behind them! Even the ducks and geese in the nearby pond stopped quacking, and came waddling over to see what was going on. And I played and I played . . .German waltzes, marches, schottisches, and always. . .the polka! They seemed to love that most of all.

By the end of summer, all the animals on the farm were attending my concerts—the new little calf, with his tired mama lumbering patiently behind him. The baby colt, peeking shyly around the corner of the barn with his big brown eyes, before he came tripping over to join us. The little pigs oinking and squealing with excitement as they listened. The baby kittens, light as snowflakes, scampering around in happy circles. Even the gophers popped out of their holes to watch and listen, while Rex looked on, his tail wagging with delight.

Sometimes, on very hot days, the bunnies didn't join us. They stayed in their cool spot underneath the barn until just before the sun went down. Then, after all the other animals had gone to sleep for the night, the bunnies would come hopping out into the cool of the evening. And, as the stars twinkled in the sky, and the moon beamed down upon us, I'd play in my "barnyard ballroom" as all the bunnies bounced and skipped around together in a bunny ballet. (Could it be that was the first time anyone ever danced the Bunny Hop?)

How I loved to play for my animal audiences! Even after I put my accordion away for the night, and crept into bed, I would still be playing—in my dreams. And one night I had a dream so vivid, and so real, I can still recall it. In my dream, I seemed to be standing in the middle of a huge crowd of people, playing for them while they all smiled and laughed and applauded. The dream was so real to me that when I woke up I knew what I wanted to do in life—make music for the people of the world.

But when I spoke to my mother and father about it, they said, "Oh, no, little Lawrencell, you're much too young to think about that! First, you must stay on the farm and get tall and strong and learn how to work."

So I stayed, working as hard as I could. But I practiced constantly on my accordion. My dream never left me, and I kept hoping that someday, somehow, I could play for audiences all over the world.

Meanwhile, I continued to play for my wonderful animal friends. But then—the summer began to turn into fall. . .and then fall into winter. The weather became very, very cold, and once again snow began to fall and cover the trees and buildings with a thick coating of white. Ice covered the pond, and all the animals began to prepare for the long winter season. The concerts came to a complete halt, and I wondered, rather sadly, if they would ever come again.

But one fine day—spring returned to the farm. The trees turned green, the flowers burst into bloom, the air became soft and warmer, and there was a regular explosion of new baby chicks, and calves, and colts, and little piglets! And I wondered. Would these new animal friends enjoy a concert? Would my old animal friends remember me at all? I decided to find out.

Once again, I took my accordion and, with Rex beside me, went out beyond the barn and sat in my accustomed spot, gazing out over the wide, flat prairies. I strapped my accordion on, and began to play one of my favorite waltzes. But when I finished. . .no animals showed up. There wasn't a sound. Nothing broke the silence but the soft rustle of the wind. I sighed, and thought, "Well, I guess they've forgotten me. The concerts really *are* over now." And just for old times' sake, I swung into one of the polkas they had loved so much.

Suddenly. . .a little pink nose popped out from underneath the barn. . .and then another. . .and another. . .all twitching. . .and here came my old friends, the bunny rabbits! One after another they hopped over to me and lined up in their accustomed places. And if bunny rabbits could smile— I'd swear they were smiling at me! I know I was smiling at them! And then a bluebird came swooping over to sit on the tree stump, and a whole flock of baby chicks came rustling around the corner of the barn. Even the ducks, swimming in the pond at the far edge of our land, stopped quacking and came rustling importantly over to join us. Rex ran around in circles, barking wildly, just as if he were dancing!

Oh, how happy I was! What a wonderful, wonderful day! My animal friends hadn't forgotten me after all! And I most certainly never, ever, forgot them.

Years later, as I played for huge throngs all across the country, I'd remember those first little audiences on the farm—those dear little animals who had given me my first encouragement. . .and put the dream of music into my heart.

After I told them this story, my children would look at me with big, big eyes. And then they'd say. . ."Daddy. . .did that really happen? Did the bunny rabbits really come out from under the barn to listen to you play—and then smile at you?"

"Well, children," I'd say, "that's a secret between the Bunny Rabbits and me. And I promised them I'd never, never tell!"

And I never have. . .until this very day.

Lawrence Welk, the shy young farm boy who grew up to become a world-famous bandleader, has always had a great affection for children. His own childhood was spent on a farm in Strasburg, North Dakota, where he was one of eight children. His parents, Ludwig and Christina Welk, were German immigrants.

Life on the farm was harsh at times, but the Welk family was a loving and closely knit one. Lawrence's mother realized that her son, who loved music so much, was not meant to be a farmer. When he was twenty-one, he left the farm and started out to make his dream of a musical career come true. He had the usual rejections and hardships of a beginning entertainer, but his charm and eagerness to please won him many followers. To this day, these same qualities continue to delight his over thirty million viewers who watch his television show each week on a syndicated network of some 258 stations.

Mr. Welk gives credit to George T. Kelly for helping him achieve his professional goals, for developing self-confidence, and presenting a show that would entertain an audience. After two years with Mr. Kelly, Lawrence Welk formed his own band and began broadcasting over WNAX in Yankton, South Dakota. During the next few years his band continued to grow and reached Big-Band status with an engagement at the William Penn Hotel in Pittsburgh in 1938. During the forties, the Welk band had an unprecedented ten-year run at the Trianon and Aragon ballrooms in Chicago. In the fifties, a move to Los Angeles and a routine telecast from the Aragon ballroom on Lick Pier in Santa Monica, launched them into television and overnight success.

One reason for Lawrence Welk's continuing success, aside from his musical talents, is his deep understanding and very real affection for others. He enjoys people and enjoys trying to please them. To Mr. Welk, his Musical Family, his own family, and his fans and friends come first. But most important of all are the children, the "little ones," for whom this book is written.

Bernice McGeehan has collaborated with Lawrence Welk on all five of his books. Married and the mother of two teen-aged children, Ms. McGeehan lives in Sherman Oaks, California.

Carol Bryan is a Kansas city artist. She received the Award of Excellence from *Communication Arts Magazine* for illustrating the Hallmark book, *Benjamin Franklin*. Mrs. Bryan lives in Prairie Village, Kansas, with her husband and son. She says that she felt honored to illustrate this book.